The Boxcar Children® Mysteries

THE MYSTERY HORSE
created by
GERTRUDE CHANDLER WARNER

Illustrated by Charles Tang

ALBERT WHITMAN & Company
Morton Grove, Illinois

Library of Congress Cataloging-in-Publication Data

Warner, Gertrude Chandler, 1890-1979.
The mystery horse / created by
Gertrude Chandler Warner;
illustrated by Charles Tang.
p. cm. - (The Boxcar children mysteries)
Summary: When their grandfather arranges for them to spend two weeks
at Sunny Oaks, the four Alden children enjoy settling into the routines
of farm life but become suspicious about a mysterious horse
locked in the stables.
ISBN 0-8075-5338-7 (hardcover).
ISBN 0-8075-5339-5 (paperback).
[1. Farm life–fiction. 2. Horses–fiction.
3. Mystery and detective stories.]
I. Tang, Charles, ill. II. Title. III. Series: Warner, Gertrude
Chandler, 1890 – Boxcar children mysteries.
PZ7.W244Mvn 1993
[Fic]–dc20   93-700
                                                                CIP
                                                                AC

Cover art by David Cunningham.

Contents

CHAPTER 1

The Big Surprise

"Please, Grandfather, I don't think I can wait another minute," Violet pleaded.

"We've really been patient," Jessie said, her dark eyes wide with excitement. "Won't you tell us now?"

It was dinnertime at the Aldens'. Grandfather Alden turned to fourteen-year-old Henry, the oldest of the Alden children. "I won't keep you in suspense anymore," he said with a smile. "I have a wonderful surprise for you. Tomorrow all four of you are going on a two-week vacation."

"A vacation!" Twelve-year-old Jessie clapped her hands together and Watch, the family dog, jumped to attention.

"No, not you, Watch," Grandfather said, patting the dog's head. "You're going to stay here and keep me company."

"Why can't Watch go on vacation, too?" Violet asked. Ten-year-old Violet loved animals and hated to leave their pet behind.

"I'm afraid Watch would get in the way," Grandfather said patiently. "And he might frighten the other animals."

"The other animals?" Benny asked. "Are we going to a zoo?"

Grandfather Alden laughed. "No, but you're going to a place with a lot of animals. You're going to a farm."

"A farm?" Violet looked curious.

"What kind of a farm?" Henry asked. He and his sisters and brother were orphans. They had been living in a boxcar, when their kind Grandfather Alden found them and gave them a real home. Since then they had enjoyed lots of fun vacations in different places.

"It's called Sunny Oaks," Grandfather said, settling back in his chair. He poured a cup of tea and stirred it thoughtfully. "It's a working farm, and the owners are very nice people with two young children. Mr. and Mrs. Morgan need to earn some extra money, so they've opened their farm to visitors."

"What will we do there?" Jessi asked. "We don't know anything about farming."

"Oh, but you will," Grandfather said with a chuckle. "That's why this vacation will be so much fun. You'll learn new things, and you'll meet new people. You'll do everything the Morgan children do. You'll live in a bunkhouse and share in the chores."

"A bunkhouse. Yippee!" Benny shouted. "I'll be a cowboy and ride the range." He pulled the reins on an imaginary horse and galloped around the room.

Grandfather turned to Violet. "And I happen to know that the Morgans keep a few horses on the place."

Violet beamed. She loved horses. "Grandfather, thank you!" She jumped to her feet and threw her arms around his neck.

When the Alden children went upstairs to their rooms to pack that evening, they found another surprise. Grandfather, with the help of Mrs. McGregor, the housekeeper, had bought them new clothes for their vacation.

"Look what I found!" Benny said to Henry. He unwrapped a pair of bib overalls, and a pair of sturdy leather boots. He fished out a red bandana and tied it around his neck. "I'll look like a real farmer now."

"You certainly will," Henry agreed. "These will be our work clothes for the next two weeks. I wonder what the girls will wear?"

Jessie stuck her head in the doorway, dressed in an identical set of bib overalls and a cotton T-shirt. "Violet and I have the same outfits," she said proudly.

"Now don't stay up too late tonight," Mrs. McGregor went on. "You're supposed to be on the road bright and early tomorrow morning."

Violet nodded happily and raced back to

her room to pack. She could hardly wait for it to be morning. She was going to spend two whole weeks on a real farm with horses. What a perfect vacation!

The sky was streaked with pink the next morning as Grandfather and the Alden children piled into the family station wagon. Watch poked his head out the rear window, yipping with excitement.

"He thinks he's going on vacation, too," Jessie said.

"Don't worry about Watch," Grandfather told her. "I'll make sure he gets plenty of treats while you're away."

"There's an extra box of dog biscuits in the pantry," Violet reminded him.

Grandfather smiled. "I'll remember that. And I'll play with him in the garden every night after dinner."

"Good," Benny said. "He'll like that."

The station wagon kicked up clouds of dust as they rolled along narrow country roads. A little while later, Henry said, "It's not much further now." He looked at the map. "You should turn left at the next junction, Grandfather."

"Look, there's a sign for the farm!" Jessie said, leaning forward.

"Oh, it's pretty," Violet said. The name Sunny Oaks was burned into a circle of polished wood ringed with bark.

"I bet we're going to wake up everybody," Benny said sleepily from the backseat. "No one gets up this early."

"Farmers do," Henry told him. "They get up at the crack of dawn to start their chores. I bet they've already had their breakfast and are feeding the animals."

"We're here!" Jessie sang out a few minutes later.

Grandfather turned slowly onto a dirt path bordered by towering oak trees. In the distance was a two-story white farmhouse, an enormous red barn, and a silo. There were several small sheds and a long, flat building that looked like a log cabin.

"That must be the bunkhouse," Henry said as they approached the main house.

"Look at all the animals!" Violet cried.

"Pigs and cows and goats and chickens . . . "

"Take a look at the pasture over there," Henry said. He pointed to a green field bordered by a split rail fence. "I can see five horses grazing."

"Can we ride them?" Benny said. He was practically jumping up and down on the seat in excitement.

"I think they're working horses," Grandfather said. He slowed down so everyone could take a closer look. "You see what broad shoulders and strong chests they have?"

"The two chestnut ones look like quarter horses," Violet said thoughtfully. She knew all about the different types and breeds from reading horse books in the library.

"Why are they called quarter horses?" Benny asked, puzzled.

"They got their name because people used to race them a quarter of a mile," Violet explained.

Grandfather pulled up in front of the main house, and a friendly-looking woman with two children hurried over to the car.

"You must be the Aldens," the woman said as Benny and Jessie tumbled out of the backseat. "I'm Cynthia Morgan, and these are my children, Danny and Sarah. Welcome to Sunny Oaks." She wiped her hands on her apron, and Violet noticed that she had a spot of flour on her nose. "You'll have to excuse me, I had to whip up an extra batch of biscuits this morning."

"We've missed breakfast. I knew it!" Benny said.

Danny, a red-haired boy of twelve, laughed. "Don't worry. I saved a couple of extra biscuits. They even have butter and strawberry jam on them." He reached into his pocket and pulled out two biscuits wrapped in napkins. "My mom makes the best biscuits in the whole world."

Benny munched happily on the biscuits while Grandfather helped Henry unload the suitcases. Violet said a shy hello to Sarah Morgan, who looked about ten years old.

"My husband wanted to greet you," Mrs. Morgan said, "but he's busy in the barn. One of our dairy cows, Sheba, had a fine calf last night."

"A newborn calf!" Violet cried. "Can we please see it?"

Mrs. Morgan smiled. "Maybe this afternoon," she promised. "But right now, I think Danny and Sarah should help get you settled in the bunkhouse."

"I think that's about it, Grandfather said, lifting a knapsack out of the backseat. Watch circled excitedly, sniffing the ground. "C'mon, boy," Grandfather said. "You and I are going to head back home and leave everyone to their chores." He hugged each of the children in turn. "Have fun, children."

"Thank you, Grandfather," Jessie and Violet chorused. Henry and Benny waved as Grandfather started up the station wagon. Watch was sitting proudly in the front seat next to him as they drove down the long winding road. Each of the children was thinking the same thing: How lucky we are to have such a wonderful grandfather!

CHAPTER 2

Daisy

"Have you ever been on a farm before?" Danny Morgan asked.

"Not really," Violet said shyly. "But all of us love animals. That's why our grandfather gave us this vacation." She stopped to look at a baby goat, wearing a bell around its neck.

"That's Jezebel," Danny said. "She gets along with all the animals, especially the horses. We let her sleep right in the stables with them because it calms them down. You can play with her later, if you want."

"But first we have to get you settled in the bunkhouse, and then we have to get back to our milking," Sarah said briskly. "The cows don't like to be kept waiting." She led the way across the yard to the long flat building they had spotted from the car.

"This looks just like something out of a cowboy movie," Benny said happily. The bunkhouse was made out of logs and had a narrow porch with wooden chairs.

Sarah laughed. "It's not fancy, but our guests seem to like it. The family in the room next to you brought four kids." She opened a rough oak door with black hinges and everyone trooped inside. The room was small, but cozy, with two sets of bunk beds, two wooden dressers, and a brown-and-orange braided rug. There were Indian blankets on the beds, and Violet noticed several horse prints on the paneled walls. There was a tiny bathroom with a Mexican tile floor connected to the bedroom.

"I love it," Jessie said, testing one of the beds.

"I get the top bunk," Benny said, scrambling up the ladder.

"Just don't fall out of bed in the middle of the night and wake us up," Henry teased him.

"After a day at Sunny Oaks, nothing will wake you up," Danny said with a laugh. "We keep our guests really busy, you know."

"Just come out when you're ready and Dad will give you your chores for the day," Sarah said. "We keep the list posted in the kitchen."

"Danny," Violet said hesitantly, "do you think I could see one of the horses up close?"

Danny beamed. "Sure. You can help me groom Oliver and clean his hooves."

After Danny and Sarah left, Benny bounced up and down a few times on his bed. This was going to be one of the best vacations ever!

"You kids look like you're ready for some hard work," Mr. Morgan said later that morning. He leaned against a pitchfork and mopped his face with a bandana. He was a tall man with a deep suntan, and he looked at the children carefully. "Now who wants to do what?"

"They've never been on a farm before, Dad," Sarah said quickly. "Maybe we better pick the chores for them."

Mr. Morgan rubbed his hands together and squinted at the sun. "Well, let me see. I'd like to finish the plowing before it gets too hot," he said. "Henry, would you like to ride in the tractor cab with me?"

"You bet!" Henry said eagerly.

Benny's face fell. Riding in a tractor didn't sound like a chore. It sounded like fun! "Aw, Henry, you have all the luck." He ducked his head and scuffed the dirt with the tip of his boot.

Sarah laughed. "Don't worry, Benny, I've got something special for you to do, too."

"You do?" His face lit up.

She nodded. "We're going to weed the garden together."

Benny liked gardening. He always helped Mrs. McGregor with the flower beds in

Grandfather's yard. But still, it didn't sound like as much fun as riding a tractor.

"You'll like it," Sarah promised. "Last year, I raised a giant squash that won a ribbon at the state fair."

"Violet offered to help me with the milking," Danny spoke up. He looked at Jessie. "If you help us, it will go twice as fast."

"I'd love to," Jessie said, pleased.

"And then maybe tomorrow we can all groom Oliver together," Violet told her. She knew that her sister loved horses almost as much as she did.

The barn was big and airy and smelled like fresh straw. Several black-and-white dairy cows looked up from their stalls and mooed when they saw Danny approaching.

"They know it's milking time," Danny explained. He picked up a wooden stool and reached for a strange-looking machine that had a lot of knobs and plastic tubing.

"What's that?" Jessie asked.

"It's a milking unit. If you hand me that pail over there, I'll show you how it works."

He plunked himself down next to the nearest cow. "We hook it up like this," he said, attaching a stainless steel cup to one of the cow's teats.

"Does that hurt her?" Violet asked worriedly.

Danny looked surprised. "No, it doesn't hurt her at all. The cup is lined with rubber and you just hook it up to each one of her teats. There's a vacuum pump in the machine that draws the milk right out."

"Do you milk her every day?" Jessie spoke up.

"Twice a day." He stopped to pat the cow on her flanks. "This is Dinah. She's the oldest cow we have, and she's my favorite." Violet watched in amazement as a stream of white liquid flowed through the plastic tubing into the pail. The cow turned her head and rolled her brown eyes at Danny.

"She likes you," Violet said softly.

A calico cat crawled out from behind a bale of hay and rubbed against Danny's leg. "Her name is Patches," he said. "She loves milking time. Just watch what she does." Suddenly

Danny lifted the tubing and milk arced through the air. Patches stood on her hind legs to catch the warm milk in her mouth. "That's enough, now, Patches," Danny said, replacing the tubing in the pail. Patches carefully licked the milk off her whiskers and curled up in a patch of sunlight.

"Can we try it now?" Jessie asked.

"It's all yours." Danny handed her the stool.

Jessie was very nervous the first time she tried milking Dinah, but it was easier than she thought. Dinah turned around to stare at her, but then she quickly relaxed and went back to munching hay. "You're next, Violet," she said to her sister.

Violet milked a cow named Jennifer, who tried to kick over the milk pail. "Did I do something wrong?" she asked in alarm.

"No, that's just one of Jennifer's tricks." Danny shook his head. "She's been doing that since she was a calf and I've never been able to figure out why."

Violet and Jessie milked eight more cows

that morning. When the last one was finished, they looked at each other and smiled. "Well, I learned something new today," Violet said.

Jessie laughed. "Me, too. I learned it's easier to get milk out of a bottle."

At noontime, the Aldens gathered for lunch outdoors with the other farm guests. It was a bright, sunny day, and everyone settled down at long picnic tables in a leafy grove. Jessie and Benny helped Danny and Sarah pass out box lunches, and Benny couldn't resist taking a peek inside. Fried chicken, potato salad, biscuits, and peach pie! How did Mrs. Morgan know these were his favorite foods?

Sarah put pitchers of iced tea and ice-cold milk on the table, and Jessie made sure there were enough jelly-jar glasses to go around. One of the other guests was a thin, dark-haired woman named Ms. Jefferies. Henry tried to talk to her a couple of times, but she seemed bored by everyone and everything. When Henry asked her how long she had been at Sunny Oaks, she smiled tightly.

"Two days. And it feels like two years," she said coldly.

Violet sat next to a shy little girl named Daisy. Daisy had long blonde pigtails and looked about seven years old. At first, Daisy barely looked up from her lunch, but Violet tried to be friendly.

"Is this your first time on a farm?" Violet asked. Daisy nodded. She seemed very timid, and Violet wondered why she was so nervous. "It's fun, isn't it?" Violet went on.

"I guess so." Daisy looked doubtful. "I wish my parents could have stayed with me, but they had to help Grandma. She's selling her house and moving into an apartment." She stared at her plate. "I'm not used to being on my own."

"What did you do today?" Violet asked, hoping to get her talking.

"I fed the chickens." She managed a little smile. "The baby chicks are really cute. They live in their own little house until they're eight weeks old."

"Maybe I'll see them tomorrow." Violet paused. "We did a lot of fun things this morn-

ing. I milked some cows, and my brother Henry rode a tractor."

"A tractor?" Daisy frowned. "That's very dangerous. You could get in a bad accident and get hurt."

"He was with Mr. Morgan," Violet explained. "And I don't think it was dangerous at all."

"You never know what can happen," Daisy insisted. "I went skiing last year and broke my leg in three places. I missed a whole six months of school." Her eyes welled with tears, and she looked like she might start crying any minute.

"That's too bad," Violet said sympathetically. "But there nothing to be afraid of here."

"But I feel so lonely all by myself," Daisy said.

"Not anymore," Violet said gaily. "I'll make sure you meet my sister and brothers after lunch. Now you have four new friends!"

* * *

After an afternoon of hard work, the Aldens were hungry when dinnertime came. Dinner at Sunny Oaks was served family-style, and the farm guests gathered at two long tables set up in the Morgans' dining room. Benny was happy to see a big bowl of butter beans. "I helped pick those," he said proudly.

"And the black-eyed peas and tomatoes," Sarah reminded him. "You've had a hard day."

Benny gave an enormous yawn. "I never thought a vacation could make me this tired," he said, and everyone laughed.

Mr. Morgan passed a basket of biscuits before sitting down. "How did you like riding on the tractor, Henry?"

"It was great," Henry said, reaching for a second helping of mashed potatoes. "You feel like you're up in the sky!"

"I'll teach you to drive it, before you leave," Mr. Morgan promised. "Do you remember how many gears it has?"

"Eight forward gears," Henry said promptly. "And three reverse ones."

"It sounds scary," Daisy said in a little voice.

"No, it's not. There's a kill button," Henry told her. "You just press it if something goes wrong, and the tractor stops right away."

It was early evening when the Aldens finally headed back to the bunkhouse, and Benny was half asleep. "Let's walk by the stables," Violet suggested. "Maybe we'll see Oliver up close."

"I think all the the horses are already in their stalls for the night," Henry said. "Sarah said her father was going to round them up while we were having dessert."

"Well, we can at least try," Violet said. She didn't want to go to sleep without getting a glimpse of Danny's horse.

When they swung by the stables, Mr. Morgan was unloading bales of hay from a flatbed truck into the stable. Violet heard some soft whinnying sounds from the half-open door, and she hurried over.

"Mr. Morgan, can we help you?" she pleaded. "We'd love to see the horses."

For the first time, a frown flitted across

Mr. Morgan's face. "I don't think so, Violet. You'd best go on to the bunkhouse for a good night's rest."

"But we're not tired, and we could help you," Jessie said. Benny gave a loud yawn and she nudged him in the shoulder.

"You've done enough work for one day," Mr. Morgan said flatly. He seemed uneasy, and Jessie wondered if something was wrong. After they said good night, she turned to Violet.

"I wonder why Mr. Morgan wouldn't let us help him with the horses. Do you think we did something to annoy him?"

Violet shook her head. "I don't think so. I think he's just tired. Don't forget, he's already put in a fifteen-hour day."

"And he has to do it all over again tomorrow," Henry chimed in. "Starting bright and early."

"Poor Mr. Morgan," Jessie said.

Benny gave another giant yawn and stumbled into the bunkhouse. "Poor us!" he mumbled. "Now I know why they call it a *working* farm!"

CHAPTER 3

The Mystery Horse

"That's right, Jessie," Danny said encouragingly the next morning. "Use short strokes with the dandy brush, and don't be afraid to press hard." Jessie and Violet were helping Danny groom a horse named Oliver. He was a large Appaloosa with colorful markings and striped hooves. They were working in the north pasture, and Jessie suddenly noticed Daisy watching from a few yards away. "Are you sure you don't want to help?" Jessie offered. "It's a lot of fun."

Daisy shook her head. "He might kick me."

"Oliver's a gentle horse," Jessie told her. She paused, resting her arm on Oliver's gleaming flank. "I have an idea, Daisy. How would you like to comb his mane when we're finished? You can even braid it if you like."

Daisy's eyes lit up. "Maybe," she said slowly. "If you promise to hold him still."

They had been working for over half an hour when Danny realized he had forgotten Oliver's hoof pick. "I'll run back and get it," Violet said.

The stable was cool and dark as Violet hurried past rows of empty stalls to the tack room. All the horses were supposed to be outside grazing, and she was surprised to hear a soft whinnying sound inside. Puzzled, she retraced her steps and found that one stall was closed and padlocked. She put her ear to the sturdy wooden panel and heard more whinnying. Why was one horse left all alone? And why was there a padlock on the door? She quickly grabbed the hoof pick and headed back to the pasture. She was very curious.

When Violet returned to the pasture, she found Danny and Jessie using a soft brush to clean Oliver's legs. "The area below the knees and hock is very tender," Danny was explaining. "Always use a brush with soft bristles or a towel."

Violet was happy to see that Daisy had edged a little closer and was watching them intently. She handed Danny the hoof pick and said, "There's one horse left all by himself in the barn. Do you have any idea why?"

Danny shrugged. "Maybe he just felt like staying in his stall today," he said vaguely.

"On a nice sunny morning?" Jessie asked in surprise. "But you said that horses love to be out in the field!"

Danny ducked his head, working on Oliver's leg. "I didn't mean — " he began, and then he stopped. "It could be that he's sick. Or something."

"Shouldn't someone check on him?" Violet asked.

"I think Dad will," Danny told her.

"But you can't even see him," Violet said. "The stall is closed and padlocked."

"I'm sure he's okay," Danny said. "I think we should get back to work now." He looked very uncomfortable, and the girls knew that he wanted to change the subject.

"Okay," Violet said. "What should we do next?"

"Oliver's feet, but I'll give you a tip first. Never just grab a horse's hoof and try to pick it up." He slid his hand slowly down Oliver's shoulder to his fetlock. "Run your hand over him first, like this. This gives him a little warning, and he'll know what to expect."

Violet noticed that Oliver seemed to get the message because he shifted his weight to his other three legs. Danny picked up Oliver's hoof and motioned to Violet. "Use the hoof pick, but be really gentle."

"I'll do my best," Violet said. Oliver didn't seem to mind at all, and she cleaned away clumps of mud and several large pebbles that were lodged in his hoof.

When they had finished, Jessie turned to Daisy. "He won't look really pretty until you comb his mane," she said.

Daisy hesitated. "How will I reach it?"

"You could sit on his back," Danny offered.

"No!" Daisy backed away.

"Wait, I have a better idea." Jessie reached out her hand. "I'll sit on Oliver and hold you in my lap. You'll be the one who combs him. Okay?"

Danny squatted down. "Just step on my shoulder, Jessie, and swing yourself up on his back. Then I'll hand Daisy up to you."

A moment later, Jessie found herself high above the ground on Oliver's back. Oliver stood very still, and Jessie patted him on the neck. When Danny handed Daisy to her, she found that the little girl was trembling.

"Don't be scared, Daisy. Danny has Oliver tied good and tight. He's not going anywhere."

Daisy relaxed then and began combing Oliver's thick, dark mane. She giggled and looked down at Violet. "You know something? This is fun!"

* * *

At lunchtime, Violet told Henry about the horse in the padlocked stall.

"It just doesn't make sense." They were eating chicken-salad sandwiches under the shade of an oak tree near the main house. "I asked Danny about it, but he didn't have much to say." She raised her eyebrows questioningly. "What do you think?"

"It's true, the horse might be sick," Henry suggested. "Or maybe he's very difficult to handle."

Violet forgot about the horse when Benny and Jessie plopped down on the grass next to them, talking excitedly.

"I rode on the tractor this morning," Benny said proudly. "Three times." He held up three fingers. "First we mowed the hay, just like it was a lawn. Then we raked it, and then we . . . " He stopped and frowned. "I forgot what came next."

Sarah hunkered down next to them. "We baled it, Benny. Remember? Now the hay is in nice square bundles."

"Oh, yeah," he said happily. "There must

be enough hay for a million horses."

"Not the way our horses eat," Sarah said. "Oliver eats twelve pounds a day."

"Twelve pounds?" Benny sputtered.

"Sometimes even more. Don't forget, he weighs almost a thousand pounds. That's half a ton."

"Wow." Benny was awed.

Then Jessie told about feeding a baby lamb with a bottle. Violet's mind went back to the horse in the locked stall. Somehow, she had to find out which horse was in there — and why.

After dinner and a Monopoly game at the main house that evening, Violet decided to walk by the stables on the way to the bunkhouse.

"You're not going to see anything in the dark," Henry told her. "Everything's closed up by now."

"I just want to take a quick look," Violet insisted. "You can go on, if you want."

When they reached the stables, they spotted a single light on, way in the back.

"That's where the stall is," Violet said

quickly. "The one with the padlock on it."
She turned to Henry. "I'm going to go in
there." She carefully slid open the stable
doors and stepped inside. Henry, Jessie, and
Benny were right behind her. They walked
softly over a thick carpeting of hay.

Suddenly Mrs. Morgan appeared from the
depths of the barn.

"What are you kids doing in here?" she
demanded.

"We're just — we came to see the horses,"
Violet stammered. She peered over Mrs.
Morgan's shoulder and noticed that the door
to the last stall was open and light was
streaming onto the stable floor. There was a
scuffling noise, and suddenly Mr. Morgan
emerged from the stall, leading a beautiful,
chestnut-colored horse. The horse was tall
and slender, and it pranced gracefully with
its head held high.

Mr. Morgan stopped dead in his tracks and
glanced nervously at his wife. "What are they
doing here?"

"They came to take a look at the horses,"
she said. Her words came out in a rush, and

Violet knew that something was wrong.

"Well, this isn't a good time," Mr. Morgan said slowly. "You'd best come back in the daytime, when they're all out in the pasture."

"But this horse never goes to the pasture," Violet said. She was surprised that she had the courage to speak up because she was usually very shy. "He never goes anywhere, does he? You keep him locked in the stall.

Mr. and Mrs. Morgan exchanged a long look. "That's because he's very high-strung," Mr. Morgan said slowly. "He gets nervous when he's around other horses, so we keep him by himself as much as possible."

"What's his name?" Henry asked.

"His name?" Mrs. Morgan repeated. She glanced at the horse, who was tossing his mane from side to side. He had gentle brown eyes and a white star on his forehead. "Star. His name is Star."

"Wow! I'd sure like to ride him!" Benny said.

"I'm afraid this horse isn't for riding, son," Mr. Morgan said gently. "I'll make sure Danny gives you a ride on Oliver tomorrow."

He glanced at his wife. "And now I think you had all better get on back to the bunkhouse. Before you know it, the sun will be up and it'll be time for chores."

An hour later, back at the bunkhouse, Violet was too restless to sleep. She kept thinking about Star. She poked Jessie, who was sleeping in the top bunk.

"Do you think the Morgans were telling the truth about that horse?" she whispered.

Jessie yawned. "I don't know. Why would they lie to us?" She propped her chin in her hand and stared down at her sister.

"I don't know," Violet said thoughtfully. "But something just doesn't make sense. Star didn't seem high-strung at all, and it seems mean to keep him cooped up like that."

Jessie shrugged. "The Morgans would never be mean to an animal."

"That's true," Violet admitted. She had seen how much they liked the farm animals and how carefully they tended them.

"So if they're keeping him by himself, it must be for his own good." Jessie pulled the covers over her head. "Now go to sleep."

CHAPTER 4

Chore Time!

The next morning after breakfast, everyone rushed over to check the "Chore List" that Mr. Morgan posted on the pantry door.

"We've got kitchen duty," Jessie said to Benny.

"Sarah and I've got something called . . . mulching," Violet said.

"Henry and I will be pitching hay this morning," Danny said, bending down to pull on his heavy rubber boots.

"Do you and Henry get to ride in the tractor?" Benny asked.

"Afraid not." Danny tossed Henry a pair of thick work gloves. "Here, put these on. You'll need them because the bales of hay are really scratchy."

Everyone trooped outside to start their chores, and the kitchen was quiet as Benny and Jessie began clearing away the breakfast dishes. Suddenly Mrs. Morgan appeared carrying a giant black cooking pot. She set it carefully on the stove and smiled at the children. "You'll find some clean aprons at the bottom of the pantry," she said, tying an apron around her waist. "You'd better put them on, so we can get started right away."

"Started with what?" Benny asked. He wasn't sure he wanted to put on an apron.

Mrs. Morgan looked surprised. "Didn't anyone tell you? This is a very special day. We're making jams and jellies for the Cooperstown Fair."

Benny grinned. Jams and jellies? Things were looking up.

"Sunny Oaks always wins ribbons for its

preserves," Mrs. Morgan said proudly. She thumbed through her recipe book. "I think we'll start with ginger-peach jam," she said thoughtfully. "If you'll get me a dozen or so peaches from that bushel basket by the door, we'll get started."

"I helped pick these!" Benny exclaimed. He filled his arms with peaches and dumped them on the counter.

"That's right, you did," Mrs. Morgan said. "Everything we enter in the fair is grown right here at Sunny Oaks."

Benny was thrilled. It seemed amazing that "his" peaches could end up in a jar of jam!

"How do we get started?" Jessie asked.

"We need to peel about three pounds of peaches," Mrs. Morgan said. She filled the cooking pan with water and turned on the stove. "If we put the peaches in boiling water for a minute, the skins come right off."

They worked steadily for the next half hour. The kitchen was bright and sunny, and they hummed as they worked.

After the peaches were peeled and

crushed, Benny added lots of sugar, a little
lemon juice, and some candied ginger. Jessie
added a package of pectin to make the jam
thicken and stirred the big pot on the stove.

"I'll show you how to melt the paraffin,
Jessie, but you have to be very careful," Mrs.
Morgan warned. "The trick is to do it slowly,
and watch it every second."

Jessie picked up a sheet of hard, waxy ma-
terial. "It smells like a candle," she said,
surprised.

Mrs. Morgan nodded. "That's how we're
going to seal the jars of jam," she explained.
Jessie plunked the sheet of paraffin into a pan
and watched as it slowly turned to liquid.

"I think the jam is ready," Benny spoke
up.

Mrs. Morgan peered into the cooking pot
and nodded. "It looks perfect, Benny. I'll
pour the jam into these glass jars, and then
we'll seal them with melted paraffin."

With Mrs. Morgan's help, Jessie poured
hot paraffin on top of each of the jars of jam.
The liquid paraffin immediately hardened
into a thick white crust, like ice on a lake.

"Wow! It's like magic," Benny exclaimed.

Mrs. Morgan lifted up one of the jars. "Looks like a winner to me. You and Jessie did a great job."

A little while later, Jessie was surprised to hear a soft tapping on the door.

"That's Lamby," Mrs. Morgan said. "If you want to feed her, Jessie, Benny and I will start making sandwiches for lunch."

"I'd love to," Jessie said eagerly. She hurried to the refrigerator where Danny kept Lamby's bottles. Since her mother had died, the baby goat had to be fed with milk supplement four times a day. Jessie warmed Lamby's bottle under hot water from the tap, and rushed to the back door. Lamby was waiting impatiently. The moment Jessie sat on the steps, Lamby nuzzled her hand, eager to start on her bottle. Jessie patted her downy fur, while Lamby guzzled contentedly. Jessie was happy, too.

Meanwhile, Violet was learning all about mulching.

"*Mulch* is such a funny word," she said to Sarah. "I thought it would be a lot messier than this."

"Maybe you were thinking of *muck*. Mucking out the stalls is a *really* messy job," Sarah told her. "Mulching isn't so bad. And it keeps the weeds away." She and Violet were spreading mulch around rows of yellow wax beans and black-eyed peas. They had just finished three rows of blueberry bushes and five dozen pepper plants.

"You mean it keeps the weeds from growing?" Violet asked.

"That's right," Sarah said. "On big farms, they have mechanical mulchers. They lay strips of black plastic along the ground between the plants. But Dad likes the old-fashioned way. He thinks that there's nothing better than a mixture of grass clippings, leaves, and wood chips."

Violet thought about the scene in the barn the night before, and wondered if she should mention it to Sarah. Would Sarah tell her the truth about Star? She was positive that there was more to the story than Mr. and

Mrs. Morgan had told her. She was wondering how to bring it up, when Sarah interrupted her thoughts.

"It's noontime," she said, glancing at the blazing sun that was high in the sky. "I'm ready for lunch, how about you?"

Violet nodded as her stomach rumbled. "I'm more than ready!"

In the meantime, Henry and Danny had been pitching bales of hay from a flatbed onto a conveyer belt that carried them to the barn loft. The square bales were much heavier than they looked, and Danny pitched one every five seconds. Henry found it hard work.

"I think we've done enough for the morning," Danny said. He didn't even seem tired, and Henry wondered if he was quitting early on his account.

"Are you sure?" Henry asked.

"I'm sure," Danny said, jumping down from the truck. "We could pitch hay all day and still not finish the job."

"Why do you need so much of it?" Henry

asked. As far as he could tell, there was enough hay in the loft to last forever!

"It goes a lot quicker than you think," Danny explained. "The cows eat twenty pounds of hay every single day during the cold months, and the horses eat hay, too." He gestured to the fields behind the barn. "It takes a whole acre of hay just to feed two of our cows for the winter."

"I understand," Henry said, wiping his face with his bandana. He was glad that he had worn gloves. The bales of hay were spiky and had scratched his upper arms.

"We always stop working at noontime, anyway," Danny explained. "The guests need a break and so do we." He glanced at Henry who was rubbing his aching arms. "Don't feel bad, Henry. My arms hurt, too!"

When Jessie finished feeding Lamby, she discovered that the kitchen was empty. Mrs. Morgan and Danny had already passed out box lunches, and everyone was eating outside at picnic tables covered with bright red-and-white-checked cloths. They had left Jessie's lunch on the kitchen counter — a cheese-and-tomato sandwich, a glass of lemonade, and a thick wedge of chocolate cake.

She rinsed out Lamby's bottle and was about to bring her lunch outside when a magazine rack caught her eye. Would Mrs. Morgan mind if she borrowed a magazine to read while she ate her sandwich? Probably not, she decided. She thumbed through the pile and settled on a new issue of *Horse Sense*. Like her sister, she loved horses. She picked up her cheese sandwich and carried it to the kitchen table.

Jessie read about a Thoroughbred named Swaps, a Kentucky Derby winner. The article explained that the Thoroughbred is the result of many generations of careful breeding and is one of the fastest horses in the world. She finished the article and was flipping through the magazine when she gasped in surprise. There was a full-page picture of Star, the horse she had seen in the stable last night!

Except his name wasn't Star, according to the magazine. It was Wind Dancer. Jessie's hand trembled as she took a closer look.

Wind Dancer was a beautiful chestnut-brown, with a white star on his forehead — just like Star. Yes, she was almost positive that Wind Dancer and Star were the same horse. But why would the Morgans change his name? And what would he be doing at a place like Sunny Oaks?

The caption beneath the picture said that Wind Dancer was a famous racehorse, and had a wonderful future ahead of him. He came from a distinguished line of racehorses. He was sixteen hands high and weighed eleven hundred pounds. Violet remembered the way the chestnut Thoroughbred had pranced into the barn, his head held proudly. He was every inch a champion and he knew it.

The question was: did the Morgans know it? And if they knew who he really was, why did they lie about him? Violet rolled up the magazine as tightly as she could and headed outside. She had to find Henry and the others and tell them what she had discovered.

CHAPTER 5

Stop, Thief!

Jessie was relieved to find Henry, Violet, and Benny sitting apart from the group, under the shade of an apple tree. They had finished eating, and Henry was whittling a chunk of white oak with his pocketknife.

"You missed lunch," Benny said the moment Jessie sat down.

"I ate inside," she said hurriedly. Then she showed them the magazine. "Look what I found in the house." She flipped to the picture of Wind Dancer and waited for their reaction.

"Oh, what a great horse," Benny said.

"Hey, that's funny," Violet said. "He looks a little like that horse we saw last night."

Henry leaned over for a closer look and then shook his head in amazement. "He looks exactly like the horse we saw." His eyes met Jessie's. "They could be twins."

"I think it *is* the same horse," Jessie said. "The Morgans call him Star, but he's really Wind Dancer. He's a champion racehorse."

"Do you really think so?" Violet asked. She peered at the magazine again. "You know, I think it *is* the same horse. But what's he doing at Sunny Oaks?"

"Maybe the Morgans kidnapped him," Benny said. "Or horsenapped him."

"I don't think so," Henry said slowly. "It could be they don't know who he really is. Maybe they're boarding him for someone."

"But it seems like they're hiding him," Violet said. She still hated the idea that the chestnut horse was cooped up all alone in the barn, whoever he was. "And I didn't believe it when they said they had to keep him away from the other horses."

"Racehorses are always around *lots* of other horses," Jessie pointed out.

"That's right," Benny said, his eyes wide. He was getting more excited by the minute. He loved solving mysteries!

"What should we do?" Violet's soft eyes were serious. "Should we say something to the Morgans?"

Henry thought for a moment. "Not just yet," he said finally. "Let's give it a little time and see what happens. And let's try to get a look at that horse again."

"Good idea." Jessie was about to say more, but she spotted Daisy racing across the yard toward them.

"Hey, Jessie and Violet!" the little girl shouted. "Want to come with me? I'm going to feed Oliver." She held up a bag of sliced apples and raisins, Oliver's favorite treat.

Jessie and Violet exchanged a look as they got to their feet. "It looks like she's not afraid

of horses anymore," Jessie said. Violet
smiled.

It was mid-afternoon when Mr. Morgan
stopped Henry on his way to the cattle shed.
"Need to talk to you for a minute, son," the
farmer said.

"Sure," Henry answered.

"I need a little favor. Mrs. Morgan wants
to go into town to set up a booth for the fair.
Daisy and the kids are coming with us, and
Ms. Jefferies went for a walk around the lake.
I wondered if you'd look after things here
for me."

"I'll be glad to," Henry said. "Is there anything special you want me to do?"

Mr. Morgan started to say something and
then stopped. "Well, not really. Just keep an
eye on the farm, that's all." He nodded and
moved off before Henry could ask any more
questions. Puzzled, Henry headed for his last
chore of the day, pitching fresh straw into
the shed.

An hour later, Henry was enjoying a tall
glass of lemonade when he looked up in surprise. A car pulling a horse trailer was rum-

bling up the main road. Mr. Morgan hadn't said anything about visitors. Henry quickly crossed the yard and stood in front of the main house. But the car roared past him, blowing up clouds of dust. It was headed straight for the stable!

Henry took off at a run, and nearly collided with Violet and Jessie who were carrying a burlap bag of chicken feed between them.

"What's your hurry?" Jessie said, laughing. She lost her grip on the bag, and some chicken feed spilled on the ground.

"No time to explain," Henry gasped. "Just follow me." He was panting when he reached the stable, and he took several deep breaths. The car had pulled right up in front of the stable, and two men were trying to open the padlocked door.

"Wouldn't you know it? It's locked up tight," one man said disgustedly to his partner.

"I told you to bring the crowbar, Hank. Only a fool would leave a stable unlocked."

"Well, we'd better think of something

quick, before they get back," the man named Hank said. "It looked like they were heading into town, but we don't know how long they'll stay there."

Henry decided it was time to speak up. "May I help you with something?" His tone was polite, but firm.

"Who are you, boy?" Hank looked questioningly at Henry.

"I'm Henry Alden." Hank edged closer, but Henry stood his ground. He noticed that both men were tall with dark hair, and they were dressed casually. The one who hung back was wearing expensive black cowboy boots with silver toes.

"What do you want?" Henry asked. He knew without turning around that Violet and Jessie had come up behind him.

There was a long pause while the two men looked at each other. Finally the one with the silver-toed boots moved toward the children. "We're here to pick up one of the horses," he said casually.

"Which one?" The words were out before Violet even realized she had spoken.

"Why, the big chestnut one, little girl," Hank said. He smiled, but Violet thought his eyes looked hard and cold. "Do you know which one we mean?"

Violet shook her head. Of course she knew which horse he was talking about, but she decided to say nothing.

"How about you?" Hank moved past Henry to stand in front of Jessie. "Have you seen a big chestnut horse with a star on his face?" Jessie shook her head, and the man threw up his hands in disgust. He turned to his partner. "Well, now what do we do, Ryan?"

Ryan tried the padlocked door again. The aging wood creaked a little, but the lock held. "There must be some way in here," he muttered. He walked back to Henry. "That just leaves you. I bet you could figure out a way to get in the stable. Maybe you even have a key."

Henry didn't flinch. "Why are you here?" His voice was strong, but his heart was beating fast.

"Oh, we should have explained that,"

Hank said. "We're here . . . " He paused and glanced at Ryan.

"We're here to take one of the horses to the veterinarian. The big one with the star . . . he's got a bad foot."

"The veterinarian?" Mr. Morgan hadn't said anything about a horse going to the vet's, and Henry was more suspicious than ever.

"Well, you'll have to come back tomorrow," Henry said firmly.

"Now that's not such a good idea," Ryan said thoughtfully. "The poor horse must be suffering. He really should be treated right away."

Violet glanced at the horse trailer behind the car. It was burgundy-colored and there was no name on it. "What's the name of the veterinarian?"

Hank scratched his head. "Well, that's easy. It's Doc, uh, Doc . . . "

"Doc Henderson," Ryan said smoothly. "Maybe you've heard of him."

Violet shook her head. She was suspicious, too. What did the men want with Wind Dancer?

Jessie turned as Benny scampered over to them. He looked at the shiny horse trailer. "Neat!" he exclaimed. "Is there a horse inside?"

"Not yet," Hank said. "I don't suppose you know how to get into the stables, do you?"

Benny looked at the padlocked door and shook his head. "No, you'll have to wait until the Morgans get home. They should be here any minute."

Violet wanted to hug him. That was exactly the right thing to say!

Hank gave a worried look to his partner. "Maybe we should come back another time," he said, backing toward the car.

"I think we'll have to," Ryan replied. He had his car keys in his hand and seemed eager to be on his way.

"That would be a good idea," Henry said firmly.

He stared at Henry for a long minute. "We'll be back." He was scowling and his voice was cold.

The moment the car rumbled back down

the drive, Violet turned to Henry. "What was that all about?" she asked. "Do you think they were here to kidnap Wind Dancer?"

"Something's going on," Henry told her. "We have to let the Morgans know right away. Wind Dancer could be in real danger."

As soon as the Morgans pickup truck pulled up in the driveway, all four Aldens hurried over. Mr. and Mrs. Morgan were busily unloading some bags of grain from the truck.

"Well, it looks like we have a welcoming committee," Mrs. Morgan said, smiling.

"We have something really important to talk to you about," Henry told her. "In private."

Mr. Morgan looked serious. "Come inside the house, children." He waited until everyone was settled in the den. "Now what's this all about?"

"We know about Wind Dancer," Jessie blurted out.

"You call him Star, but we know who he really is!" Violet chimed in.

"Some men were here today to steal him!"

Benny said, his eyes wide. "But we stopped them just in time."

Mrs. Morgan put her hand to her mouth. "Oh, no!" she cried.

"Slow down," Mr. Morgan said. "Now, Henry, start at the beginning and tell me exactly what happened."

Henry told him about the men trying the padlocked door, and he gave a good description of the car and the horse trailer. When he finished Mr. Morgan shook his head.

"I guess I should have been honest with you last night," he said. "I lied when I said the horse was named Star."

"Then Star really *is* Wind Dancer!" Jessie said. "I knew it the moment I saw his picture in *Horse Sense*."

"We're keeping his identity a secret to protect him," Mrs. Morgan told her. "He was nearly stolen last month, and his owners wanted a nice safe place to board him for a couple of weeks. Sunny Oaks seemed like the perfect spot." She shook her head sadly. "But now the thieves are after him again."

"What can we do to help?" Henry asked.

"Just don't tell anyone what you know," Mr. Morgan said. "And I'll keep him hidden in that back stall as much as I can."

"Doesn't he ever get out?" Violet asked. "I feel so sorry for him."

Mr. Morgan smiled at her. "Now don't worry about him. I make sure he gets some exercise. I take him out every other night on the old bridle path that runs around the pond." He paused. "I suppose I'm taking a chance, but I wait until it's dark, so no one can spot us."

"We'll have to be more careful than ever, now that there's been a second attempt," Mrs. Morgan pointed out.

"We'll do whatever we can to help you," Henry offered.

"You can count on us!" Violet piped up.

"I'm glad that you know the truth," Mrs. Morgan said. "And thank you for what you did today. That took some quick thinking."

"Yes, you kids did a great job," Mr. Morgan added. "Wind Dancer is safe, thanks to you."

CHAPTER 6

The Barn Raising

A few days later, Benny was working with Sarah in the vegetable patch when he had a great idea. Why couldn't *he* try for a prize at the Cooperstown Fair? Jessie and Violet had already decided to make a blueberry pie for the baking division, and Henry had offered to help Danny with his apple cider project. Unless Benny thought of something fast, he'd be left out!

"Sarah," he said, looking up from his weeding, "what do you have to do to win a prize at the fair?"

Sarah picked a ripe green pepper and tossed it into her basket before answering. "Well, you have to make something or grow something. But whatever you do has to be the biggest or the best." She peered at him from under her straw hat. "Why?"

"I wanted to enter something," he said firmly. "But I haven't figured out what."

"Well, just look around you," she told him. "You could make a sweet potato pie . . . " She laughed when she saw his expression. "It's good. It tastes just like pumpkin pie."

Benny shook his head.

"Hmmm, let me see. You could make a batch of pickled watermelon rind," Sarah suggested. "Mom would help you."

"Ugh. That sounds even worse!" Benny said.

"It's delicious," Sarah told him. "You cut up the rind in little pieces and cook it. When you're finished, it tastes so sweet, you'll think it's candy. We make it every year."

Benny sighed. This was going to be much harder than he had thought. "Maybe I could grow something," he suggested.

"You don't have much time. The fair is only three days away," Sarah reminded him. "Well, maybe you could find something that's ready to harvest. If it looks really big and healthy, you could pick it and give it a try."

"I could? Are you sure nobody would mind?" Benny was beaming. He had spotted a giant cantaloupe the day before that would be perfect.

"I'm sure," Sarah said. "If you can find it, you can enter it."

Later that afternoon, Benny was weeding chives in the herb garden with Daisy. She didn't seem to know anything about herbs, and he had to point out the chive plants from the rows of basil and parsley.

"I'm entering corn dolls in the fair," Daisy said proudly. "I'm using a clothespin for their body and corn leaves for their skirts. They look just like hula dancers. What are you going to enter?"

"I've got a big cantaloupe," he said. "I bet it will win a blue ribbon for me."

"Really? How big is it?" Daisy asked.

"Big," Benny said. "And it's growing bigger by the second." He squinted at the sky like a real farmer. "All I need is a couple of more sunny days."

Daisy shook her head. "You don't need the sun. Someone told me cantaloupes grow twice as fast in the moonlight."

"They do?" Benny asked

"I think that's what they said," Daisy replied.

"Wow. I hope there's a full moon tonight," Benny said. He went back to the chive plants but he couldn't stop thinking about that cantaloupe. Would it grow twice as big on a moonlit night? There was only one way to find out.

Benny waited until everyone was asleep in the bunkhouse that night before tiptoeing to the window. A big silver moon hung in the sky, spilling beams of light across the yard.

"Bingo," he said softly. Still in his pajamas, he quietly pulled on his boots and went out onto the porch. He was heading toward the cantaloupe patch when he saw someone crossing the yard toward the stable. Who

would be out at this time of night? he
wondered.

He crept past the main house and crouched
down behind a wheelbarrow as the figure
came into view. It was Ms. Jefferies, the
snooty woman who didn't like being on a
farm! What was she up to?

Benny waited until she had passed him,
and then he followed her, being careful to
stay out of sight. He barely had time to duck
behind a maple tree when she stopped suddenly in front of the stable. To his amazement, she pulled out a camera and began
taking pictures! After a few minutes she
looked over her shoulder nervously, and then
darted around the side of the barn.

Benny was stumped. What should he do
next? If he followed her, she might spot him,
but he had to find out what she was up to!
Maybe she was heading to the back stall to
steal Wind Dancer!

As Benny rounded the barn, Ms. Jefferies
turned around, but he quickly scrunched
down behind a bale of hay so she didn't see
him. He heard the camera clicking again and

again, and he couldn't resist taking a quick
peek. Now she was taking pictures of the
padlocked stall door! She *must* be after Wind
Dancer, he thought in alarm. He was so
shocked, he lost his balance. When he
grabbed the bale of hay to steady himself, a
bundle of fur flew through the air and landed
on his shoulder. Patches, the barn cat, had
been sleeping in the hay!

There was a loud meow, and Benny heard
Ms. Jefferies gasp in surprise. Holding his
breath, he took a chance and peered around
the corner of the hay bale. It was too late.
Ms. Jefferies was already running through
the yard, back to the bunkhouse.

Benny got up and dusted himself off as
Patches wound around his legs. He reached
down and patted her on the head as she
purred. "You'll never make a detective,
Patches," he told her.

A few minutes later, Benny was tiptoeing
across the bunkhouse porch, when Jessie
opened the door. She was clutching her robe
around her, and looked worried.

"Where were you?" she asked. She pulled

him inside where Henry and Violet were waiting.

"You're not going to believe this," he began, and told them about Ms. Jefferies. When he finished, everyone was quiet for a minute.

"Maybe it's not what we think," Jessie said.

"But she was up to something!" Benny scooted up the ladder to his bunk and sat down on it. "I know it!"

"We're not sure of that," Henry said slowly. "All she did was take a few pictures. She might be an amateur photographer."

"So what are we going to do?" Violet shivered a little and pulled her comforter around her.

"Nothing," Henry said. "At least not yet. Until we have something definite to go on, let's not say a word to the Morgans."

"We wouldn't want to worry them for nothing," Jessie said.

The next morning at breakfast, Mr. Morgan surprised everyone by making an announcement. "We've been invited to a barn raising at the Tyndall farm. Anyone who wants to help, is welcome to come along. We can use the extra hands."

The Aldens immediately raised their hands. "Count us in!" Jessie said. She had never heard of a barn raising, but she knew it would be an adventure.

An hour later, after the cows were milked and the chickens fed, the Alden children piled into the back of a pickup truck for the short drive to the Tyndall farm. There was a steady stream of cars rolling along the country road.

"Looks like everyone in Cooperstown is here," Mr. Morgan said to Henry when he got out of the truck. Dozens of men and women were already hard at work sawing lumber and nailing together sturdy wooden beams.

"What's going on?" Henry asked. The Aldens followed Mr. Morgan past a man using a radial saw to trim a plank of knotty pine.

"Whenever anyone needs a new barn, everyone pitches in to help," Mr. Morgan explained. "That's the way it is in the country. We all depend on each other."

"Can we build a whole barn in one day?" Benny asked.

"We'll just get the frame done today," Mr. Morgan told him. "All the boards will be nailed together, and by sundown, we'll raise all four sides."

"So that's why you call it a barn raising," Violet said.

Mr. Morgan nodded. "Exactly. Bob and his sons can put on the roof later." He pointed to a man in jeans and a tattered cowboy hat. "That's Bob. If you kids head over that way, he'll give you each a job to do."

"Wow," Benny said softly. "He's wearing a holster, like a real cowboy."

Mr. Morgan laughed. "That's not a holster, it's a pouch to hold roofing nails."

They split up as soon as Bob gave them their assignments. Benny and Jessie found themselves working side by side. Bob had given them a tape measure and they were marking lumber and sorting it into neat piles to be sawed. It was hot, dusty work, and Jessie was glad she had worn shorts and a T-shirt.

Henry and Violet were assigned to the "kitchen brigade" along with six other Sunny Oaks guests. "We need a lot of help because Mom serves sandwiches at lunch and a big dinner at six," Joe explained. Within minutes Henry found himself peeling a mountain of potatoes and carrots while Violet rolled out pastry dough for apple pies.

The morning passed quickly, and the Aldens were happy to take a break for lunch with Mr. Morgan. They were eating ham-and-cheese sandwiches at a picnic table when they were joined by a friendly man in his late twenties.

"Are you Mr. Morgan?" he asked. "I've been hoping to catch up with you all morning. I'm Jed Owens." He sat down next to Violet.

"Ed's the name," Mr. Morgan said, extending his hand. "Are you from Cooperstown?"

"No, I'm just visiting from up north. I'm Bob's cousin."

"Well, I hope you enjoy your stay."

"I'm sure I will. Cooperstown is a nice

place." He hesitated. "You know, I'm hoping to get a few days' work before heading back home. Could you use an extra hand at Sunny Oaks?"

Mr. Morgan looked him over carefully. "I can always use help around the place. What kind of farming do you do?"

"Well, a little of everything. Dairy, poultry, vegetable . . . and I'm good with horses."

"Sounds good to me," Mr. Morgan said, getting up. "You can start tomorrow morning. Check in with me around five-thirty."

"I'll be there," Jed said. "And thanks."

It was barely sunset when Mr. Morgan nudged Benny on the shoulder.

"It's time to raise the sides, so you'd best stand clear."

"Raise the sides?" Benny looked up, puzzled. He had been squatting in the dust, pulling bent nails out of a pine board.

Mr. Morgan laughed. "This is the moment we've all been working for. Look around you, boy. You're standing right smack in the middle of where the new barn will be!"

"I am?" Benny gulped. He took a slow look around, and realized that the four walls had been assembled on the grass, and men were attaching guide ropes. In just a few minutes the barn would be standing by itself!

"Wait on the sidelines," Mr. Morgan cautioned as he went to lend a hand. "We don't want any accidents to happen."

"No sir!" Benny agreed, and he scampered over to join Jessie and Violet. They watched in amazement as Mr. Tyndall shouted to the workers, and right on cue, all four sides suddenly started to rise from the ground.

"Steady now!" Mr. Tyndall yelled. Everyone started clapping and laughing as the sides stood straight up, pointing skyward.

"Look at that!" Benny said. "It's a real barn, now, except for the roof."

Jessie and Violet hugged each other. It felt like a real celebration!

At the end of the day, all four Aldens, tired but happy, piled into the back of the Morgans' pickup truck. Violet craned her neck for a last look at the barn frame, which stood out against the darkening sky.

"Just think," she said, "we helped build a real barn today."

"We sure did," Benny said sleepily. He nestled his head against her shoulder and was about to drift off when Bob Tyndall hurried over to the truck.

"Hey, little guy," he said, nudging Benny's shoulder. "I've got something for you. A little souvenir to remember us by."

Benny sat up straight and watched in amazement as Bob took off the tan leather pouch that looked like a holster and handed it to him.

"You're giving it to me to keep?" Benny said, thrilled.

"It's all yours. It's even got some roofing nails inside."

"Wow!" Benny immediately fastened the pouch to his belt. "I'm going to wear it every day," he said. As the truck rolled down the road to Sunny Oaks, Benny ran his hand over the smooth leather pouch. This was a day he would never forget!

CHAPTER 7

A Day at the Fair

The following afternoon, the Aldens finished their chores early and rode into town with Mr. Morgan and Sarah.

"I always stop at the post office for the mail while Dad goes to the hardware store," Sarah said. "Then we both head straight to Hilary's for chocolate ice cream sodas."

The post office was crowded, and Benny spotted Ms. Jefferies picking up a large manila envelope at the counter. "Look who's here," he whispered. "And for once, she's smiling!"

Ms. Jefferies turned quickly toward the door and nearly bumped into Sarah and Violet. "Sorry — oh, it's you," she said, recognizing the children.

"Hi, Ms. Jefferies," Sarah said politely. "We would have been glad to pick that up for you." She pointed to the manila envelope, and Ms. Jefferies shook her head and turned pink.

"No, I . . . it's nothing," she said.

"We always pick up mail for our guests," Sarah went on. "It's really no trouble — "

"I told you no thanks!" Ms. Jefferies blurted out. She clutched the envelope to her chest and hurried out of the post office.

Benny looked up in surprise. "What was she so mad about?"

Sarah shrugged. "Maybe she was just in a hurry. She might have a lot of stops to make."

Benny smiled. "Like at Hilary's, for a chocolate ice cream soda," he said, and everyone laughed.

Later that afternoon, Jessie was delivering fresh towels to the bunkhouse guests. She tapped lightly on Ms. Jefferies's door. When no one answered, she let herself in and left the towels on the sturdy pine dresser. She started to leave when she noticed a pile of photographs on the dresser. Suddenly she realized that they were photographs of Wind Dancer!

But how did Ms. Jefferies get them? Wind Dancer was hardly ever out of the stable! Something very strange was going on. But Jessie didn't want Ms. Jefferies to come in and think she was snooping. She quickly moved toward the door. But in her hurry, she stumbled over Ms. Jefferies's briefcase. Setting the briefcase upright, she noticed the gold initials on the top. "A.S.F.," she said softly. "Something's not right . . . " She shook her head and quietly let herself out.

Jessie waited until after dinner to tell Henry and the others what she had discovered. They were as surprised as she was.

"You're sure it was Wind Dancer in the photographs?" Henry asked. He kept his voice low because they were sitting on the front porch of the main house. He and Violet were perched on the porch railing, and Benny and Jessie were rocking on a handmade swing.

"I'm positive. And the funny thing is that they were just like the pictures you see in magazines."

"What do you mean?" Violet asked.

Jessie thought for a moment. "Well, they were really clear, and they were taken from all different angles."

"Maybe Ms. Jefferies is a good photographer," Henry said.

"But that still wouldn't explain how she managed to get close to Wind Dancer," Violet pointed out. "He's always locked up during the day."

"That's true," Jessie agreed. "And what about the initials on the briefcase?"

"Maybe it belongs to someone else and she stole it," Benny piped up. "Or borrowed it."

"Wait, I just thought of something," Violet said, her eyes big. "What if Ms. Jefferies isn't using her real name?" Everyone turned to look at her. "What if she's using a phony name at Sunny Oaks?"

"That would definitely mean she's up to something," Henry said grimly.

No one said anything for a long moment. Then, finally, Jessie broke the silence.

"What should we do?" she whispered.

"We'll just have to wait and see what she does next." Henry looked very serious. "And we'll try to watch her as much as we can."

Since there didn't seem to be anything else to say or do about Ms. Jefferies, Henry and Benny went inside to play checkers, and Jessie and Violet went for a walk.

"Let's go by the stable," Violet suggested. "I have half an apple I saved for Oliver."

A few minutes later, the girls were happy to see that the stable was unlocked and Oliver was happily munching hay inside his stall.

"Hey, Oliver," Violet said as the horse ambled over to greet them. She handed him the apple. Suddenly a sharp noise from the interior of the barn made her jump in surprise.

"What's that?" Jessie cried.

"Sorry to frighten you, girls," a voice said in the shadows. "I think I just knocked over a pitchfork." Jed Owens, whom they'd met at the barn raising, strolled out casually from the back of the barn. Jessie and Violet exchanged a look. He was coming from Wind Dancer's stall! What was he up to?

"What are you doing here?" Violet asked.

"Oh, just locking up," he said vaguely. Violet knew something was wrong. Danny had said that Mr. Morgan always locked up the stable. He *never* would give the keys to someone else.

Jed started to head out the door but changed his mind and stopped by Oliver's stall instead. "Hey, that's funny," he said, pointing to a small bundle of fur sleeping in the straw. "How did that goat get in here?"

"That's Arnold," Jessie said, surprised. "He always sleeps with the horses."

"He does?" Jed laughed. "Doesn't he know he's a goat?"

"Of course he does. But farmers like to have goats sleep in the horse stalls. They calm the horses down."

"They do?" Jed looked amazed.

"Didn't you know that?" Violet asked.

"Sure . . . I guess I just forgot." Jed ran his hand through his hair and looked embarrassed.

"We'd better be going," Violet said. Suddenly she wanted to get back to the main house. First she had felt suspicious of Ms. Jefferies, and now Jed Owens!

It was very late that night when Benny crawled out of bed and went quietly outside. Henry had been teaching him all about the constellations, and he wanted to take another look at the night sky. "There's the big dipper," he said to himself. "And the North Star and the Seven Sisters . . . " Suddenly he was distracted by two beams of bright light flashing by the pond. He rubbed his eyes and looked again. The lights disappeared for a minute and then swung in a big arc. Maybe it was a ghost! Or a spaceship!

He hurried inside and shook Henry's shoulders. "Henry, wake up," he pleaded. "There are some really scary lights by the pond."

"You're imagining things. Go back to

sleep," Henry mumbled into his blanket.

"But the lights . . . I saw them. Honest!"

Henry sat up and peered out the window. "I can't see anything out there."

"They come and go," Benny insisted.

Henry rumpled his brother's hair. "There's nothing to be afraid of. It's probably all those ghost stories Mrs. Morgan told tonight. Let me know if you see more lights, though."

"Okay." Benny sighed and climbed the ladder to the top bunk. Mrs. Morgan had told some scary ghost stories earlier that evening around the camp fire. But this was different. He really *had* seen those lights!

It was bright and sunny two days later, and everyone was excited over the Cooperstown Fair. Benny ate his breakfast in record time, and then raced over to the vegetable patch to pick his prize cantaloupe. He had decided to leave it on the vine until the very last moment so it would grow as much as it could. As he trudged back to the main house, he shifted his tool belt around his waist, and glanced idly toward the pond. He *knew* he had seen lights at the pond the other night. But what did they mean?

Violet and Jessie helped Mrs. Morgan load pies and jams into the back of the pickup truck, and Henry helped Danny pour his apple cider into brown jugs. When everything was ready, Mrs. Morgan took a final look around the kitchen. "Have we forgotten anything?" she asked the Aldens.

"Plenty of paper plates and plastic forks," Benny piped up.

Mrs. Morgan looked puzzled. "What for?"

"So we can eat the pies when the judges are finished with them!"

Mrs. Morgan smiled. "There's plenty of food at the fair, Benny. And don't worry. I'll save you a slice of every one of our pies that wins a prize."

"And even the ones that don't," Benny said, and everyone laughed.

Half an hour later, the Morgans pulled up into a grassy area next to the Cooperstown County Fairgrounds.

"Here we are!" Sarah sang out. "And

look how many people showed up!"

"There's a good turnout this year," Mr. Morgan said approvingly. He pointed to dozens of colorful display booths set up in neat rows. The narrow aisles between the booths were jammed with visitors, and children scampered everywhere.

The Aldens scrambled out of the back of the pickup truck, and Benny gave a low whistle when he spied the top of a Ferris wheel. "Wow! I didn't know there would be rides. It looks just like a carnival!"

"They always have a few rides at the fair," Sarah told him, "but the homemade goodies are the best part."

The Morgans waved to a young girl leading a pinto pony out of a horse van. "She's showing her horse in the ring for the very first time," Sarah said to Violet. "If you want, we can go to one of the competitions. They go on all day long."

"That would be wonderful." Violet clapped her hands together excitedly.

"Remind me to stop by Mrs. Ames's booth," Mrs. Morgan said. "I'd like to buy some of those needlepoint key rings she makes." She smiled at Jessie. "They make wonderful Christmas gifts."

"Let's go, everybody," Mr. Morgan said. He unloaded Danny's cider from the back of the truck and handed Benny his cantaloupe. "Who's going to carry the pies?"

"The Aldens will help me," Mrs. Morgan said. "Take two each, and nobody drop them!" she pleaded.

Violet helped arrange the sparkling jelly glasses and pies on a long picnic table covered with bright blue felt. Several people stopped to buy pickled watermelon rind and blueberry jam.

"We have to pick one of these apple pies to be judged," Mrs. Morgan said to Violet. "Which one do you think is the best?"

Violet looked at the pies and pointed to one with a delicate latticework crust. "That one," she said proudly. She remembered how Mrs. Morgan had taught her to cut the pie crust in thin strips and lay them crisscross over the apples.

"Please keep an eye on things while I drop it off," Mrs. Morgan said, heading for the judges' table.

Violet was busy for the next hour as people lined up to buy preserves. She had just sold the last jar of peach-ginger preserves when she spotted a tall, dark-haired man walking across the fairgrounds. There was something familiar about his face, and she squinted, concentrating. She knew she had seen him before, and then suddenly it came to her. He looked just like one of the men who had tried to kidnap Wind Dancer! She tried to get a better look at him, but someone drove a pickup truck down the midway, blocking her view.

She needed help, but who could she ask? Henry had gone back to Sunny Oaks to fetch more cider, and Jessie was helping Sarah sell corn dolls. Then she spotted Benny, clutching a giant wad of pink cotton candy, standing right in front of her!

"Benny!" she cried. She dashed around the table, hugging him in relief.

"What's going on?" His face was sticky

from the candy and he tried to wriggle away.

"I need you to help me," she said, bending down so her face was close to his. "I think I just saw one of the men who tried to steal Wind Dancer."

"Really? Are you sure?" Benny gulped.

"I think so, but I have to stay here at the booth, so I need you to find out. He's wearing a cowboy hat, and he's over by the leather goods booth. It's the place with all the belts and saddles. If you hurry, he'll probably still be there."

Before she could say another word, Benny handed her his cotton candy and scooted away. His heart pounding, he zigzagged past a boy leading a Shetland pony, and nearly got caught in a line of prize hogs being moved into a pen. Still running, he darted past a popcorn stand and skidded to a stop when he spotted the leather goods booth. There was the man in the cowboy hat! His back was turned to Benny, and he was talking to another man.

Benny sneaked up to the side of the booth and dropped to his knees. He waited until no one was watching and then dove under the heavy cloth that covered the display table. Luckily it drooped almost all the way to the ground, and he knew that no one could see him. The two men were still talking, and Benny crawled quietly toward the sound of their voices.

"I think we should do it at night," one of the men was saying. "There are too many people around the stable during the day."

"You're right. But I'd sure like to get the key to that stall. It would make things a lot easier."

Benny cautiously peered out from the narrow slit between the cloth and the muddy ground. His nose was just inches away from a pair of black leather cowboy boots with silver toes. Those were the same boots the man named Ryan had been wearing the day he tried to steal Wind Dancer!

Benny scurried backward until he was at the end of the display table and then bolted out from underneath. He ran all the way back to Violet, who was telling the Morgans about the man she'd spotted.

"It's them!" Benny gasped to Mr. and Mrs. Morgan and Violet. "I recognized the cowboy boots."

"Let's go see," Mr. Morgan said quickly to his wife. "The children should stay right here."

The next half hour passed slowly as Violet and Benny waited for the Morgans to return. Finally Mr. Morgan appeared and rubbed his forehead wearily. "It's no use," he said. "We checked the leather goods booth and walked all around the fairgrounds. They're nowhere in sight."

"Oh, no," Benny said. "Maybe they saw me and ran away."

"Don't worry about it, Benny," Mr. Morgan said. "You did a good job tipping us off. Now we know they're going to try again, and we'll have to be extra careful."

At sunset, the Alden children piled into the back of the pickup truck for the ride back to Sunny Oaks. Benny was thrilled because his cantaloupe had won a third-place ribbon, and Jessie and Violet were very excited that their pies and jams had won prizes.

Wind Dancer was on everyone's mind, though. That night, back in the bunkhouse, Violet finally mentioned him. "It's scary to think those men are still around," she said. "And that they're going to try again."

"If only we could have caught them today, the whole thing would be over," Henry said.

"Maybe not," Jessie spoke up. "There might be other people at Sunny Oaks who are working with them."

"Like Ms. Jefferies?" Benny asked.

Jessie shrugged. "It could be. Or what about Jed Owens? He said he's always worked on farms but he sure doesn't know anything about horses."

"Why do you say that?" Henry was suddenly interested.

"Violet and I ran into him in the stable and he was surprised to see a goat there. I had to explain that Arnold sleeps in Oliver's stall lots of times."

Everyone was quiet, thinking the same thing. There was going to be another attempt on Wind Dancer. But who? And when?

CHAPTER 8

Fire!

The next evening, the Morgans invited the guests to a wienie roast at the old pond. "We do this every year right after the fair," Sarah explained to Jessie. "Everyone roasts their own hot dogs, and then we sit around the camp fire and sing. I guess you could say it's a Sunny Oaks tradition." She and Danny were setting out crocks of baked beans and platters of potato salad on a long picnic table. Benny plunked down a giant vat of sauerkraut, and Violet arranged jars of mustard and relish.

"I think the fire's just about ready," Henry said. He and Mr. Morgan had built a camp fire from hickory logs and tossed a few pine-cones on top to give it a woodsy scent.

"Mmm, it smells good," Violet said.

"It'll make the hot dogs taste even better," Benny piped up. As usual, he was starving!

"Why don't you help yourself, Benny?" Mrs. Morgan said. "The rest of the guests are starting to wander over." She handed him a hickory switch and he stuck a hot dog on the top. "Just remember to hold it over the flames, not in them."

Benny accidentally let his first hot dog turn black on one side, but he was so excited that he ate it anyway with plenty of mustard and ketchup. The second one was even better because he had figured out how to rotate the hot dog so it cooked evenly.

"This is a beautiful spot," Jessie said to Danny. The sun had already set over the pond, and they were sitting under a willow tree, balancing paper plates on their laps.

"This is where Dad takes Wind Dancer for his exercise," Danny said, keeping his voice low. "You see that trail between the pine trees over there?" Jessie nodded. "It's the old bridle path, and it runs all the way around the pond. Wind Dancer gets a good workout, and it's really safe. No one can spot them."

"I hope you're right," Jessie said, a little shiver going down her back. She knew that Wind Dancer would never be completely safe as long as the two horse thieves were around.

After Benny had finished a second helping of blueberry cobbler, he stood up and stretched. A twinkling of lights at the edge of the pond caught his eye and he nudged Violet. "Hey, look at the lightning bugs," he said. "There must be a hundred of them over there in the forest."

"Oh, they're pretty. I love the way they blink on and off." Violet scrambled to her feet. "Let's go over and see them." After they carefully threw away their paper plates, Violet and Benny headed for the dense pine forest that ringed the old pond. The grown-ups were having coffee, and they knew it would be another hour or so before the camp songs started.

As they started to walk around the pond, Benny taught Violet what he had learned about the constellations. "You see that little group of stars all stuck together? That's the Seven Sisters," he said proudly. "Henry said it's one of the easiest ones to spot. That's the very first constellation he taught me."

"Oh, I think I see the Big Dipper," Violet said. "Or is it the Little Dipper?" She brushed aside a pine branch and noticed that the sharp needles clung to her sweatshirt.

Benny tilted his head to one side. "No, you're right, it's the Big Dipper. I like that one, because it looks just like its name. Some of the other ones are hard to pick out."

"That's funny," Violet said in a strange voice. She was staring at the blanket of pine needles on the ground.

"What's wrong?"

"Look over there," she said, tugging at Benny's arm.

Benny shrugged. "It looks like the pine needles are all mushed down, that's all."

"Those are tire tracks," she said.

Benny stared, his eyes round. "I knew it! Henry said I was dreaming, but I knew I was right." Quickly, he told Violet about seeing lights around the pond one night. "They weren't ghost lights, they were headlights!"

"Someone was out here snooping around," Violet said. Her voice was shaky. "Do you think we should follow the tracks and see where they lead?"

Before Benny could answer, a shout went up from the direction of the camp fire. "Fire!"

"That sounded like Henry," Violet said, grabbing Benny by the arm. "We better see what's up!"

They started to race back to the picnic area and then realized that everyone was heading in the opposite direction.

"Oh, no," Benny wailed. "The fire must be back at the farm."

"It's at the stable!" Violet shouted. She pointed to a thick coil of black smoke above the roof of the stable.

By the time they had dashed back to the stable, the smoke was gone and a small group of people had gathered around Jed Owens.

"What happened?" Violet asked Danny.

"It was a false alarm," Danny said. "But it's a good thing Jed was here to take care of it."

"So the stable wasn't on fire after all?" Benny asked. He stepped into the middle of the circle and looked right at Jed Owens.

"Luckily it was just a tin drum filled with garbage," the young man told him. "Somebody must have tossed a match into it, and some dried twigs and leaves ignited."

"That was a careless thing to do," Mr. Morgan said gruffly.

"It sure was," Jed agreed. "I'm just glad that I caught it in time."

Benny was puzzled. "But how come you were here? Didn't you go to the cookout?"

Violet thought that Jed looked a little uncomfortable. "No, you see, I wasn't feeling very well, and I decided to stay in my room and rest. I had just started reading, when I thought I smelled smoke. So I ran right outside and put out the flames."

Violet had a nagging feeling that something was wrong, but she couldn't put her finger on it. Everything Jed said made sense, but why did she feel so uneasy?

In the middle of the night, the answer came to her, and she sat straight up in bed. "The pine needles!" she said out loud.

"What?" Benny sat up sleepily and rubbed his eyes.

"Nothing," she said quickly. "Go back to sleep." She waited until he fell back on the pillow and then sat up, her chin cupped in her hand. Now she knew why she had felt something was wrong the whole time Jed Owens was talking. His sweater was covered in pine needles, just like her sweatshirt! The story about reading in his room was a lie. She knew exactly where he had been — in the pinewoods, spying on them! But what was he up to? And who had set the fire?

CHAPTER 9

Danger Strikes!

The following morning, Violet told Henry and Jessie about the tire tracks she and Benny had spotted near the old pond.

"You're sure they were fresh tracks?" Henry asked.

Violet shrugged. "I think so."

"They might have been left by visitors," Jessie suggested. "Maybe the Morgans drove down there after dinner. The pine forest looks so pretty in the moonlight."

"The pine trees!" Violet exclaimed. "I almost forgot to tell you something else important." She quickly explained about seeing pine needles on Jed Owens's sweater.

Henry frowned. "I don't know what to say, Violet. The pine needles don't really prove anything one way or the other. Maybe he was in the woods earlier in the day."

"Maybe," Violet said doubtfully.

"Anyway, we can't do anything unless we're really sure," Henry added.

Later that morning, Violet spotted Mr. Morgan waving to her from the cornfield, and she hurried over to him.

"Violet," he said pleasantly. "You're just the person I've been looking for. I've got a surprise for you."

"You do?"

Mr. Morgan glanced over his shoulder and said in a low voice, "I just found out that Wind Dancer is going home tomorrow. His owners will be here first thing in the morning to pick him up."

"He's leaving? But we never got to see him up close," Violet said. She couldn't hide her disappointment. She knew she would probably never have a chance to see a real race-horse again.

"Don't worry, you're going to get your chance tonight," Mr. Morgan told her. "You can even feed him a little treat if you want."

"I can?" Violet was thrilled.

Mr. Morgan nodded. "I'm taking Wind Dancer out to the old pond for the last time, and you're all welcome to come see him." Mr. Morgan's blue eyes twinkled. "After all, if it weren't for you Aldens, he might have been stolen by now."

"We'll all be there!" She couldn't wait to tell the others.

"Oh, and why don't you bring Daisy with you? She's gotten over her fear of horses, and I think it would mean a lot to her."

"It means a lot to all of us," Violet told him. "Thanks!"

Violet hurried over to Benny, Jessie, and Henry, who were eating lunch with Daisy at the picnic table.

"You mean we'll get to ride Wind Dancer?" Benny said, munching on a ham-

and-cheese sandwich. He had taken off his tool belt and had laid it carefully on the table.

"No, I don't think so," Violet said. "We'll just watch him exercise with Mr. Morgan."

Benny's face fell. "Oh, I wanted to pretend I was a real jockey."

"Cheer up, Benny," Jessie said. "You'll probably see him trot and gallop and do all the things that racehorses do."

"Maybe Mr. Morgan will let you hold the reins," Daisy piped up. "He lets me lead Oliver in and out of his stall." Daisy giggled.

Violet smiled at her. Daisy was completely different from the shy, frightened little girl who had come to Sunny Oaks. She was happy and full of confidence.

There was a full moon later that evening when the Aldens crept quietly out of the bunkhouse. Daisy was waiting for them, a big smile on her face.

"We're really going to see Wind Dancer," she whispered, taking Jessie's hand. "I can hardly believe it."

They had crossed the yard and were just heading down the dusty path to the old pond when they spotted Mr. Morgan walking rapidly toward them.

"Hi, kids," he greeted them. "I forgot Wind Dancer's blanket, and I'm going to dash back to the stable and get it. Why don't you go ahead and see him? He's tethered to a tree at the edge of the pond."

"We'll take good care of him," Violet promised.

They walked steadily for the next quarter mile, but when they rounded the bend, they were in for a shock. The two men who'd tried to steal Wind Dancer were loading him into a horse van!

"Oh, no!" Jessie cried. "They're stealing him!"

The men turned at the sound of her voice. "C'mon, move it!" Ryan said gruffly to Hank. They quickly slammed the van doors shut and jumped into the cab.

"They're getting away!" Henry said as the men gunned the engine. He sprinted after the van, but stopped when it made a tight U-turn and headed back toward them. Jessie reacted immediately and pulled Daisy and

Benny into a shallow gully next to the path.

"I'll go for help!" Violet yelled. She darted through the woods back to the stable, her heart beating fast. She had to get to Mr. Morgan in time or Wind Dancer would be gone forever!

Meanwhile Benny wriggled free from Jessie's hand and watched the horse van roaring down the path. In just a few seconds, the van would pass them and it would be too late. Suddenly, he knew what he had to do. He scrambled out of the gully and reached into the leather pouch Bob Tyndall had given him at the barn raising. His fingers closed over the roofing nails and just as the van approached, he flung them into the center of the road. When the van passed over them, there was a satisfying pop, and Benny grinned. The nails had done their job. The van had a flat tire!

The van skidded to a stop and both men got out, looking furious. "Now look what you've done!" one of the men said to the other. "How are we going to fix it?"

"That won't be necessary," a male voice

said firmly. Jessie and Daisy watched in amazement as a figure stepped out of the woods. It was Jed Owens! Benny's mouth dropped open and he looked at Henry, puzzled. Had Jed Owens come to help them or had he come to steal Wind Dancer?

Both men turned in surprise as Jed Owens approached them. "Don't bother fixing the flat," he said in a friendly voice, "because you aren't going anywhere. Except to jail."

The thieves looked nervously at each other, and Hank started to back away. "Who are you?" he demanded hoarsely.

"Jed Owens. And you don't have to introduce yourselves. I know who both of you are. I've been watching you for a few weeks now." He looked at Benny and gave him a big smile. "That was quick thinking."

"But who *are* you?" Henry asked.

"We knew you weren't a farmer," Benny blurted out.

"You're right. I'm a private security guard. Wind Dancer's owners hired me to protect him." He grinned at Benny. "Of course, it's always nice to get a little help from my friends." Suddenly they heard a siren, and a black-and-white car with flashing lights raced down the path toward them.

"It looks like the game is up, guys," Jed Owens said to the thieves. "I hope you don't have any plans for the next few years."

Everything happened very quickly once the police cruiser pulled up. Two policemen jumped out and handcuffed the thieves, and Mr. Morgan and Violet hurried down the path to Henry and the others.

"Is everyone okay?" Mr. Morgan said.

"We're fine," Daisy piped up. "But what about Wind Dancer? Maybe he got scared by all the noise. Shouldn't we check on him?"

Mr. Morgan laughed. "We'll do that right now," he said. Suddenly he spotted Jed Owens. "Jed?" he said hesitantly. "What are you doing here?"

"It's okay," Benny piped up. "He's one of the good guys. He helped us save Wind Dancer!"

"Well, I'm glad to hear it," Mr. Morgan said. He shook Jed Owens's hand as one of the police officers approached them.

"We'll need a statement from both of you. Can you come down to the station house first thing in the morning?"

"No problem," Jed Owens said.

Mr. Morgan nodded. "We'll be there."He watched as the police cruiser pulled away with the thieves in the backseat. "Why don't we all go back to the house and have some hot chocolate? We have a lot to talk about."

Benny looked up at Jed Owens admiringly. "I have a zillion things I want to ask you."

"Why did you tell us you were a farmhand?" Violet asked.

"Were you really in the woods that night?" Jessie demanded.

"How come you kept your identity a secret?" Henry chimed in.

"Wait a minute!" Daisy cried. She stood in the center of the group and crossed her arms over her chest. "You're all so busy talking, you've forgotten all about Wind Dancer. He's all by himself in the horse van, probably scared to death."

"Don't worry, Daisy," Mr. Morgan said.

"We're going to fix that right now." He took her by the hand and led her to the van. When he opened the rear doors, Wind Dancer gave a soft whinny and turned his head. He stomped his foot, impatient at being cooped up in the van.

"Easy now, boy." Mr. Morgan's voice was soothing as he eased the champion horse down the ramp. He handed Daisy the lead rope. "He's all yours, Daisy. You hold the rope good and tight, and stay to his left shoulder, like I showed you."

"You mean I can take him back to the stables all by myself?"

Mr. Morgan smiled. "I don't see why not."

"Thanks," Daisy said softly. She patted Wind Dancer's cheek and then stepped out smartly, with just the right amount of tension on the rope. The horse trotted obediently next to her. She had never felt so proud in her whole life!

CHAPTER 10

The Mystery's Over!

"What's going on?" Mrs. Morgan looked anxious when the Aldens appeared at the main house. She was standing on the front porch with Danny, Sarah, and Ms. Jefferies. "I thought I heard a siren, and Danny said he saw flashing lights over by the pond."

"It was a patrol car," Ms. Jefferies insisted. "The police were here, right?"

"Yes, but there's nothing to worry about," Mr. Morgan said reassuringly. Ms. Jefferies edged closer to Henry. "What really happened out there?" she asked. "It was something to do with that horse, wasn't it?"

Henry hesitated and looked at Mr. Morgan who said quickly, "If you want to hear the whole story, let's go inside." Everyone trooped into the kitchen and gathered around the big oak table. Danny heated milk for hot chocolate in an iron kettle and then scooted over to the window bench. He didn't want to miss a single word!

Ms. Jefferies remained standing, her arms folded across her chest as she looked over the group. "Before you say anything, I have a confession to make," she said.

Jessie and Violet exchanged a puzzled look. A confession? Was Ms. Jefferies involved in the plot to kidnap Wind Dancer after all?

"I came here under false pretenses," she said. "I'm not really here on vacation. I'm doing research for an article."

"An article?" Mrs. Morgan said. "Are you a writer?"

"A reporter." Ms. Jefferies perched on the arm of Jessie's chair.

"I don't understand," Henry said slowly. "What are you writing? And how come you kept it a secret?"

Ms. Jefferies shrugged. "It started out as an article on farm vacations, but all that changed when I spotted Wind Dancer."

"So you *do* know about him!" Benny blurted out. "That's why you were taking pictures that night. I was hiding behind a bale of hay outside the stable."

"Was that you?" Ms. Jefferies said in surprise. "I had the feeling someone was watching me. That's why I left in a hurry."

"But how did you get the pictures of Wind Dancer I saw on your dresser? I spotted them when I brought your towels," Jessie said.

"Oh, I didn't take those pictures," Ms. Jefferies said. "Those were file photos that my editor sent me from New York." She turned to Mr. Morgan. "I thought I recognized Wind Dancer one night when you were taking him out of the stable, but I couldn't be sure. I wanted to get to the bottom of it, so

I asked ASF to send me some close-up shots of him. Once I saw the white star on his forehead, I knew it was the same horse."

"ASF?" Jessie exclaimed. "Those are the initials on your briefcase."

"Associated Feature Service," Ms. Jefferies said. "That's who I work for. I went to town to pick up the pictures because I didn't want anyone to get suspicious."

"So that's why you acted so nervous in the post office," Violet spoke up.

Ms. Jefferies nodded. "I didn't want you to see the return address. I couldn't let anyone know I was a reporter."

"Well, that clears up one mystery," Jessie said.

"But the big story is still Wind Dancer," Ms. Jefferies persisted. "What's he doing here? And what happened tonight?"

"Some horse thieves were trying to steal him!" Benny exclaimed. "But we stopped them, didn't we?" He looked very pleased with himself.

"You sure did," Mr. Morgan said. "Wind Dancer is safe, thanks to you, and the thieves are in custody." He spread his hands on the checkered tablecloth and looked right at Jed Owens. "But there's still a lot of the story that I don't understand. How do you figure in all this?"

"I was hired to protect Wind Dancer," Jed Owens admitted. "The owners asked me to stay undercover, so I pretended to be a farm-hand looking for work."

"At first, we thought you were one of the thieves!" Violet exclaimed.

"Why did you think that?" Jed asked.

"You lied to us," Violet explained. "You said you were in your room the night of the cookout, but you had pine needles stuck all over your sweater. So that meant you must have been in the woods with us."

"Pine needles?" Jed said slowly. "You'd make quite a detective, Violet. I never thought a little thing like that would give me away."

"Were you really in the woods that night?" Benny asked.

"Did you set that fire in the trash can?" Henry said at the same time.

"Yes, to both questions." Jed turned to Benny. "I saw you and your sister wandering through the forest, and I was afraid you might run into the horse thieves. I heard some suspicious noises earlier in the evening, and I had the feeling they might be prowling around the woods."

"We saw some tire tracks," Benny piped up. "That's what got us so interested."

"I know, and I couldn't take any chances. I had to do something fast to get your attention away from the old pond."

"So you started a fire back at the farm," Mrs. Morgan said.

"A small one," Jed told her. "I made sure it wouldn't do any real damage, but it would make everyone come running."

"There's something I still don't understand," Henry said. "What were you doing at the old pond this evening?"

"I knew there might me another attempt to steal Wind Dancer tonight." His expression was grim. "I wanted to warn you in time," he said to Mr. Morgan, "but by the time I got there, it was too late." He paused.

"The thieves would have made off with him, if these young people hadn't stopped them."

"A plot to kidnap a racehorse. This will make quite a story," Ms. Jefferies said thoughtfully.

"Wind Dancer's owners will be here in the morning," Mr. Morgan said. "So if you kids want to say good-bye to him, you'd best be up bright and early."

"We will be," Benny said and immediately yawned.

A bubbling sound made Danny scramble off the window seat. "The milk for the hot chocolate!" Danny said, dashing to the stove.

Moments later, Mr. Morgan passed around steaming mugs to everyone. "To the Aldens," he said, raising his mug in a toast.

"To Wind Dancer," Henry spoke up.

"The best racehorse in the whole world," Violet added.

It was barely dawn the next morning when a large silver horse trailer rumbled down the road to Sunny Oaks.

Benny and Daisy dashed to the stables,

followed by Violet, Henry, and Jessie.

Mr. Morgan had just finished adjusting Wind Dancer's blanket when the trailer pulled up to the stable door. A man and woman in their late thirties got out and smiled hesitantly at the Aldens. Mr. Morgan led Wind Dancer outside just then, and the stallion whinnied softly when he recognized his owners.

"Oh, thank goodness you're safe," the woman said, rubbing Wind Dancer's nose.

"Mr. and Mrs. Travis, these are the Aldens," Mr. Morgan said. "And their friend Daisy."

"You're the children who saved Wind Dancer," Mr. Travis said. "Jed Owens called us last night and told us all about it."

"How can we ever thank you?" Mrs. Travis asked.

"We're just happy that Wind Dancer is all right," Jessie said.

Violet patted the prize horse gently on the neck and he nuzzled her hand. "We're going to miss you," she said softly.

"Don't worry, Violet. We'll still get to see

him." Benny fed Wind Dancer an apple slice he had carefully wrapped in a napkin. "We'll watch every single race he's in."

"And next time he wins, we'll send you a picture of him at the finish line," Mrs. Travis promised. "C'mon, boy," she said, patting Wind Dancer gently on the flank, "it's time to go home."

The Aldens waved good-bye as Mr. and Mrs. Travis loaded Wind Dancer into the horse trailer and sped away from Sunny Oaks.

"Don't look so sad, Violet," Henry said. "Grandfather will be here in a few minutes to pick us up. Think of how much fun it will be to see him again."

"We have so much to tell him," Jessie agreed.

"My parents are here!" Daisy shouted. She pointed to a jeep lumbering up the main drive to the farmhouse. She raced over to greet her family and then waved to the Aldens to join them.

"These are my friends," she said, introducing each of them.

"You forgot someone," a voice piped up. Daisy turned in surprise to see Danny and Sarah leading Oliver toward them. "Don't you want to show your parents what you've learned?" Danny asked.

Daisy giggled. "Watch this, Mom and Dad!" She got up on a mounting block and put her left foot in the stirrup. Then she swung herself into the saddle.

"Are you ready?" Sarah asked.

"All set," Daisy answered. Sarah handed her the reins and Daisy rode Oliver in a wide circle around the group.

Her parents looked amazed. "I can't believe it," her father said. "We're so proud of you, honey."

"I never thought I'd see you riding a horse all by yourself." Her mother was beaming.

Half an hour later, the Aldens had said good-bye to Daisy and were waiting for Grandfather to arrive. They had already thanked the Morgans, and were sitting on their suitcases outside the main house, in the early morning sunlight.

"I'm going to miss everything about Sunny

Oaks," Violet said. "Especially the animals."

"I'll miss Mrs. Morgan's biscuits," Benny said.

"Grandfather's here!" Jessie jumped to her feet as a familiar station wagon pulled up in the circular driveway. "And look — Watch has his head out the window!"

"Grandfather, we missed you!" Benny tumbled into Grandfather's arms as soon as the car door opened. Watch hopped out of the backseat and ran in circles around the children barking happily.

"We missed you, too," Grandfather said.

"We had a lot of adventures," Henry said. He hugged his grandfather and then began storing the luggage in the car.

"It will take forever to tell you about them." Violet jumped into the backseat and pulled Watch in with her.

"We even solved a mystery," Jessie said.

"Let me tell, let me tell!" Benny pleaded.

"All right," Jessie said with a laugh. "You tell Grandfather what happened."

"Well," Benny said, "it all started with this racehorse with a star on his forehead. . . ."

GERTRUDE CHANDLER WARNER discovered when she was teaching that many readers who like an exciting story could find no books that were both easy and fun to read. She decided to try to meet this need, and her first book, *The Boxcar Children*, quickly proved she had succeeded.

Miss Warner drew on her own experiences to write each mystery. As a child she spent hours watching trains go by on the tracks opposite her family home. She often dreamed about what it would be like to set up housekeeping in a caboose or freight car — the situation the Alden children find themselves in.

When Miss Warner received requests for more adventures involving Henry, Jessie, Violet, and Benny Alden, she began additional stories. In each, she chose a special setting and introduced unusual or eccentric characters who liked the unpredictable.

While the mystery element is central to each of Miss Warner's books, she never thought of them as strictly juvenile mysteries. She liked to stress the Aldens' independence and resourcefulness and their solid New England devotion to using up and making do. The Aldens go about most of their adventures with as little adult supervision as possible — something else that delights young readers.

Miss Warner lived in Putnam, Connecticut, until her death in 1979. During her lifetime, she received hundreds of letters from girls and boys telling her how much they liked her books.